For Kirsty, Erika and Elizabeth, Stronvar and Port na Luing

KATIE MORAG AND THE DANCING CLASS
A RED FOX BOOK 978 1 862 30221 1

First published in Great Britain by The Bodley Head, an imprint of Random House Children's Books
A Random House Group Company

Bodley Head edition published 2007
Red Fox edition published 2008

1 3 5 7 9 10 8 6 4 2

Copyright © Mairi Hedderwick, 2007

The right of Mairi Hedderwick to be identified as the author and illustrator of this work has been
asserted in accordance with the Copyright, Designs and Patents Act 1988.

All rights reserved.

Red Fox Books are published by Random House Children's Books,
61–63 Uxbridge Road, London W5 5SA

www.rbooks.co.uk

Addresses for companies within the Random House Group Limited can be found
at: www.randomhouse.co.uk/offices.htm

THE RANDOM HOUSE GROUP Limited Reg. No. 954009

A CIP catalogue record for this book is available from the British Library.

Printed in China

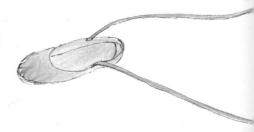

MORAG G CLASS

High Farm

The Holiday House

Mrs Bayview's

The Lady Artist's

The Redburn Bridge

The Village

Nurse's

Effie
&
Ronald
the
Road's

Mrs
Baxter's

Neilly
Beag's

The
Ferryman's

TEAS

KATIE MORAG
and the DANCING CLASS

Mairi Hedderwick

RED FOX

It was decided that it would be a good thing for the children on the
Isle of Struay to have dancing lessons.

Agnes, Fay, Sasha and the Big Boy Cousins were keen to start, especially
when they heard that Mrs Mackie would provide juice and biscuits at the
end of each lesson.

The boys chose tap and the girls ballet. But Katie Morag McColl said she
had better things to do on a Saturday morning – like getting a backy on her
mother's Post Office bike or checking the lobster creels with Neilly Beag.

But Grannie Island said that ballet would be good for Katie Morag's co-ordination. Granma Mainland had already ordered pink pumps and a leotard from a dance shop on the Mainland. She was also sewing a frilly frou-frou skirt. She longed to see her granddaughter in a pretty outfit instead of that old jumper and skirt and those dreadful wellies.

Katie Morag loved her wellies.

She dreaded the thought of ballet lessons, but
it had all been decided by the two grandmothers.

On the first Saturday, Katie Morag reluctantly put on the leotard. Granma Mainland rushed into Katie Morag's bedroom waving a cloud of frills. The frou-frou skirt!

"Oh, no . . . !" thought Katie Morag. But, "Thank you very much, Granma Mainland," she said.

"Hurry up! Don't be late! There is to be a Dance Performance on Show Day! You will look SO pretty!" smiled Granma Mainland.

Katie Morag headed unwillingly towards the Village Hall. It was boat day and all the villagers were at the pier. But all was not silent and deserted at the last house in the Village. Nurse's gate was wide open and a flock of sheep were in her garden, baa-ing delightedly as they feasted on her early lettuces.

Katie Morag tried to chase them out but *every* time they came back in before she could close the gate.

After a long time, and a lot of shouting, which she enjoyed, Katie Morag finally got the sheep out and firmly shut the gate.

Katie Morag was late for ballet class . . .

On the second Saturday, Katie Morag decided to walk to the Village Hall along the shore. There had been a big storm in the night. She was on the lookout for anything interesting washed up on the tide line.

Once she had found a Frisbee which she gave to Liam for his birthday. And then there was the terrible time when she had been in a bad mood and had kicked her old teddy into the sea. She was so lucky to find him washed up two days later near Grannie Island's house.

This particular day, there was nothing special on the tide line –
but Katie Morag just *had* to keep on looking.

Katie Morag was *very* late for ballet class . . .

On the third Saturday, Flora Ann screamed all through breakfast. It being boat day, Katie Morag very kindly offered to stay with her until Mr and Mrs McColl collected the mail and supplies for the Shop and Post Office from the pier.

For once Katie Morag didn't mind having to look after her baby sister. Grannie Island was downstairs wiping the shelves in the Shop and completely forgot it was Dancing Class day. Katie Morag didn't remind her. The boat was an hour late in arriving.

Katie Morag was *extremely* late for ballet class.

SO LATE that she missed the whole class. Agnes, Fay and Sasha had already gone home. The Big Boy Cousins were putting on their tap shoes.

"What is it like to tap dance?" Katie Morag asked.

"It's like playing the drums with your feet," replied Hector, Archie, Dougal, Jamie and Murdo Iain, clacking the metal-studded toes and heels of their shoes on the floor.

WHAT A NOISE!

Katie Morag copied them with her wellies but the sound was like a wet fish flapping in the bottom of Neilly Beag's boat.

"You have to have the metal bits," laughed Jamie.

Mrs Mackie had been listening. "Would you like to come to tap, Katie Morag, instead of ballet? I am sure Granma Mainland would get you the shoes."

Katie Morag desperately wanted to say "Yes, please!" but she couldn't *possibly* ask Granma Mainland for more dancing shoes.

That night Katie Morag was staying over at Grannie Island's.

Wearily, she told Grannie Island the whole sad story.

"Take off your wellies," sighed Grannie Island sympathetically, "and have a rest by the fire."

Katie Morag looked at her wellies. "All they need are bits of metal . . ." she said forlornly.

Grannie Island suddenly started rummaging in a cupboard. She held up a pair of dusty leather boots. "My old tackety boots!"

"Silly Grannie!" scoffed Katie Morag, a bit rudely. "They are FAR TOO BIG!"

But Grannie Island was levering the metal tacks from their soles and hammering them onto the soles of Katie Morag's wellies.

On the fourth Saturday, on the dot of 11 o'clock, Katie Morag was the first at the door of the Hall. Mrs Mackie said not a word about the rather unusual tap shoes.

"What are you like, Katie Morag?" the Big Boy Cousins groaned.

But Jamie laughed. "She's like she is. She's Katie Morag!"

Katie Morag worked really hard to catch up on her cousins.
Rehearsals had already started for the Dance Performance on Show Day.
Mrs Mackie made them practise their routine over and over again.

On the evening of the Dance Performance,
the islanders packed into the Village Hall.
The two grandmothers were in the front row;
Granma Mainland dressed up in all her finery,
looking forward to seeing Katie Morag in *her* finery . . .

Granma Mainland was so disappointed when she saw Katie Morag wearing that old jumper and skirt and those dreadful wellies – *on the stage!*

But when Katie Morag danced perfectly in time with the Big Boy Cousins and even did a solo turn in her tackety wellies, Granma Mainland had to admit that she was extremely impressed.

Katie Morag was equally impressed by the ballet performance. Agnes was Aladdin, in a blue satin bolero and baggy trousers, and Sasha was Princess Jasmine in veils of purple silk. Fay performed high wild kicks as the Genie coming out of the lamp.

At the end of the wonderful evening, the Lady Artist thanked Mrs Mackie for all her hard work and gave her a bouquet of flowers specially ordered from the Mainland.

"And I would like to thank all the dancers who worked so very hard, too," Mrs Mackie replied. "Katie Morag worked the hardest of them all!"

Afterwards, Katie Morag apologized to Granma Mainland for not telling her about missing ballet lessons and how she really liked tap dancing.

Then she said, "But Granma Mainland, I think I would like to go to both classes next year . . ."

Granma Mainland smiled her forgiveness. Maybe she would see Katie Morag in that frilly frou-frou skirt one day, after all.

"And, look," said Katie Morag brightly, "the ballet shoes I didn't use this year won't be wasted. They will make cosy liners for my wellies in the winter!"

JOIN

Katie Morag

ON MORE ADVENTURES!